THE SWIPE THAT CHANGED IT ALL

RAHUL RAM

To my loving wife, Divya, who has been my moral support from the moment we started to till now. With every success and every failure, you have stood by me as my greatest strength. This book is as much yours as it is mine.

I also want to take a moment to thank myself for believing in this dream and following it through to conclusion. Writing this book was no small task, especially as a first-time author, filled with doubts and endless questions about whether I could do justice to the story. On top of that, personal issues within my family were constantly present in my thoughts during the entire process. Rather than letting them defeat me, these challenges used to step up my determination to finish what I planned to achieve.

Today, I'm proud—not just because I've written a book, but because I've taken a step that no one else in my family has ever attempted. It's a milestone I hold, and one that reminds me how far perseverance and belief in oneself can truly take you.

Thank you, Divya, and thank you to everyone who played a part—directly or indirectly—in helping me bring this vision to life.

Contents

Acknowledgements

I would like to thank my friend **Rajavelu**, the author of **"EA-R-TH : Age of NeOlwd"** for guiding me to write this book.

I also extend special thanks to my **English teacher, Valsala Harikumar**, whose passion for teaching and dedication have had a deep impact on my life. You are one of the reasons that I started enjoying and learning the English classes. Your influence had much to do with shaping my love for learning and writing, and I'll always be thankful for the foundation you laid.

I would like to thank my friend **Vicky**, the designer of my book cover, for all the help with the designs. Thank you for the time and effort you invested in this work. I truly appreciate your patience in bearing with me through all the changes I requested repeatedly, and still provided the best possible design for my book.

Preface

This story didn't start with some complex equation or highly advanced invention. It began simply with the profound question, **"What if we could just erase all our pain of yesterday?"** That was the most understandable appeal to a power so longed for because who wouldn't want to break free from past suffering over bad mistakes, over regrets, over losses? That would be an excellent temptation to block out the pain and promise a life burdened by our darkest memories.

However, the effects of changing the memory of the core of our identities are much more complex. Memories define who we are; they represent our choices, our relationships, and the essence of our identity. There is a part of ourselves that, if changed or erased, would risk getting lost in the change. The impacts on the human spirit and those of such enduring, long-term effects are incomprehensible and immeasurable.

The further I got, the deeper the concept, immersing myself in the complexity through relationships and that which no man can truly see within a fellow human. The more I dove down, the more it became apparent that love, loss, and memories are interlocked, impacting each other.

Healing over loss is neither forgetfulness nor remembering but acceptance. Remembering and accepting the growth of love in new forms. As I delved deeper into this mindset, I immersed myself in the complexity of grief and loss through relationships and unparalleled human capacity. With this realization came Vivaan and Anaya's journey.

The story of Vivaan and Aanya shows that love is an unbreakable bond, no matter how advanced technology becomes. It is a fragile and resilient memory that subtly defines our present, even though our past is filled with pain and suffering.

Through various experiences, we celebrate how the human spirit can live, heal, forgive, and ultimately learn to love again, even after significant loss. Healing, rising above pain, and acknowledging the beauty of new beginnings transcends time, technology, and memory.

This story presents a romance with sci-fi elements and indulges in the darkest recesses of the human heart, where characters suffer enough yet find endless joy. It's not only about love; it speaks about the marks left behind on us, our decisions, and the undeniable force behind human attachment. It's about the strength of the heart, which heals even the deepest wounds through connection and creates a brighter future than the past we may have once thought defined us.

CHAPTER ONE

SHADOWS OF MEMORY

Vivaan's apartment was more than just a place to stay; it was an impressive set of wires, tools, and half-finished products. The air was full of a soft, mechanical hum, like a symphony of creation, echoing off an otherwise silent room. Vivaan had plastered every corner with blueprints and scribbled notes, taping them to the walls or pinning them to cork boards. The chaotic mosaic of a mind perpetually at work formed his sanctuary.

He had been working on a project for years: inventing a device to erase memories. Not a dream of fame or curiosity, as a teenager. Vivaan faced the misfortune of losing his parents in a car accident. That day, the accident tore his world apart, leaving him stranded in emotional ruin. Sadness clung to him like a shadow, a constant companion he could never shake off.

Over the years, Vivaan's bright, adventurous spirit had dimmed. He was an inquisitive kid who asked all kinds of questions and always took things apart to understand how they worked. His parents had encouraged his imagination, teaching him to dream big and build bigger. But the absence of them had sucked all the color from his life. The boy who used to laugh at his mistakes and celebrate his small victories was no more; a man working day and night to escape the pain replaced him.

It was no longer an inviting luxury apartment but a calm, practical place. The furnishings were minimal and functional, opting for practicality rather than comfort. In one corner, there was an irregular mattress. Vivaan rarely used the kitchen. It was often cluttered with tools rather than cookware. He scattered his leftovers everywhere, each splatter carrying a fragment of the work relics of his forgotten dream.

Vivaan often wakes up in the early mornings when the sun is barely up, but his mind is full of thoughts. After pouring himself steaming cups of coffee, he enters his own world. He would forget his hunger for meals and slumber for hours. It seemed that the machine fed on him. It was his obsession, his lifeline, and his curse. He believed with unwavering confidence that if he could erase the memories of his parent's deaths, he would finally be able to move on. He would be free.

But freedom came at a price. Years of isolation took their toll. Vivaan rarely went outside. He limited his contact with the outside world to brief barter sessions, with delivery drivers and occasional trips to the hardware store. For years, he had no meaningful conversation with anyone. The idea of forming a new relationship seemed impossible. How did he relate to others when he was trapped in the past and overwhelmed by memories that hadn't left him?

In quiet moments, when the hum of his machine was the only sound in the room, Vivaan sometimes questioned his approach. Is this really the answer? Can the device erase not only the memory of pain but also the scars it leaves behind? And if it works, who will he become? These doubts hurt him, but he pushed them aside, burying them beneath his determination and stubborn rejection. He had no choice but to lean on the machine. It was the last hope he had.

The prototype sat at a workstation in the middle of the room. Vivaan's hands shook as he worked through a tangled mess of stars and circuits that looked more like a science experiment than a significant modification, soldering connections and meticulously fixing every component. The designers strikingly crafted every part of the machine. The machine's hardware and software was intertwined perfectly. Despite this, however, the machine was not perfect. It remained a dream just out of reach, so close yet frustratingly evasive.

Vivaan was hopeful of being seen as capable of making someone's life better, or he would regret the time he spent out of place within society. No one bothered to share his burden any longer, and no one personally invested deep meaning in his suffering. He just couldn't imagine opening his mouth again or showing such weakness. It was easy to be alone, focused, and self-sufficient.

Late at night, when his exhaustion knocks him out to sleep, Vivaan would rather lie on his mattress with his eyes fixed on the ceiling. He was often haunted by visions of his parents, and his mind was flooded with the painful memories. He could hear his mother laugh and his father smile. Memories were a bittersweet double-edged sword for him. It reminded him of both comfort and agony of what he had lost, of a life he would never have again.

Sometimes, he would dream of them. In those dreams, they were alive, their faces bright and full of love, their soft voices comforting him. Yet the dream always ended with the same terrible dread of nonexistence. He woke up panting, grief heavy in his chest. Such moments fired up his determination and convinced him he had to complete the machine, whatever the cost might be.

The outside world appeared remote and insignificant to Vivaan. He did not pay much attention to time, seasons, or people's lives. His neighbors knew nothing of him except that they occasionally saw his weary face when he brought back bags while he went out shopping. To them, he was a mystery, a quiet, independent man who existed and never caused trouble. They had no idea of the battle he fought inside those walls and the daily burden he had been carrying.

Vivaan's solitary prison was not entirely unknown to humanity. There were brief and fleeting moments where he felt a small connection. The stranger's smile and the cashier's kind words reminded him that he was still a part of the world, even if he felt like an outsider. But it wasn't enough to pull him out of solitude. His suffering was unmanageable, and he was at the end of it.

CHAPTER TWO

A NEIGHBORLY COLLISION

Vivaan's life had always been neatly fragmented, like his immaculate room. His work, filled with neatly arranged books and journals, reflected his desire to control. The city outside his window was a whirlwind of sounds and activities, but he kept it all away with the walls he had erected; both in the real world and the imaginary one. That kind of life suited him, or so he thought.

That changed one Saturday morning when Aanya came out. The hallway smelled of fresh coffee as sunlight entered through the tall windows and danced on the polished wooden floors. Vivaan carried his bag and turned around to see Aanya emerge from the opposite direction, holding a tray of coffee cups that were balanced unsteadily.

It was bound to happen; one of the cups toppled spilling coffee all over Vivaan's pristine white shirt.

"Oh my God!" Aanya's eyes widened, but a soft smile left her lips. "Well, this is embarrassing. My coffee-serving skills need work."

Vivaan stiffened at her reaction. "Uh, no harm done," he muttered, pulling out a napkin to rub the stain.

"Here," she said, digging out a napkin from her pocket.

Her warm, apologetic eyes stayed on him for a moment. "I owe you a new shirt or maybe a better cup of coffee?"

Vivaan hesitated. He wasn't used to people offering to fix things for him, especially not with such casual charm. "All right," he said contemptuously, avoiding her eyes as he left.

However, she couldn't stop smiling as she stepped into the elevator. It wasn't funny at all but it felt real, like a gentle breeze might blow on a hot summer day.

The next time Vivaan saw her, she sat in the courtyard, balancing her sketchbook on her knees. The courtyard was a small generic space for the tenants, almost empty except for the occasional stray dog that wandered in. But Aanya had the rooms and studio and spread paint, brushes, and canvas pots on the bench.

Vivaan had come to collect his mail when Aanya called out his name.

"Hey, neighbor! Do you ever stop and see how nice this place is?"

He glanced, trying to figure out how to respond. "Okay. Nice, I guess."

Nice?" She repeated, as if worried. "Look at that tree over there." He waved a hand at the twisted oak tree with its fiery autumn leaves. "It looks like a living painting! And this, doesn't she look like she has stories to tell?"

Vivaan looked to where her eyes had landed. The orange tabby slumped on the bench. "It's just a tree and a cat," he said unchanged, though he envied how little he could see himself.

Aanya laughed. "You can't," she teased. "But do not worry; I will turn you into one."

They saw each other more and more frequently. Aanya's unwavering optimism and charming personality did not go amiss with Vivaan. He would always hide behind indifferent expressions.

One evening, she knocked on the door of Vivaan carrying herself a tray of cookies.

"These are for you."

"I don't eat cookies." He said the words, yet the fragrance of freshly baked cookies with chocolate made his mouth water.

"Liar," Aanya smiled, pushing the tray into his hand. "Everyone is having cookies. And you look like you need some cheer."

Vivaan frowned. "I don't need to cheer up."

He studied her and turned his head. "You wear pain like a second skin, Vivaan. But that doesn't suit you."

Her words surprised him, but he didn't let them show. Instead, he softly muttered "thank you" under his breath and closed the door.

Alone in his room, staring at the tray of cookies she left on his doorstep, it somehow felt more than any gesture.

Aanya's carefree facade disguised her endeavors. One morning, over coffee at a small café down the street, she opened up to Vivaan.

"I left my hometown because it became strangling," she said, looking out the window at the street full of people. "Everyone knew me as the girl who never gave up, always lost in her dreams."

Vivaan listened to her, surprised at her honesty. "Why does that bother you? You seem to grow up differently."

"I do," she said, her voice softening. "It felt like living in a dark shadow, and I couldn't see my light. This move was my way of stepping into the sun."

Vivaan connected with her more than she expected. "Sometimes you have to leave the shadows behind even to remember what light feels like," he said quietly. "Some of us just hide them well."

Their conversation turned out to be a turning point. Vivaan started talking openly about his struggles—his estranged family, the pressures of his job, and the loneliness he tried so hard to ignore. Aanya was stuck in his art, the story of failure, and often her doubts.

One evening, Aanya convinced Vivaan to join her at a pottery class. "Come on, it'll be fun," she said, practically dragging him out of his apartment.

Laughter filled the studio, and the scent of wet clay filled the air. Awkward and unsure, Vivaan tried to form the lump of clay in front of him.

"You're overthinking," Aanya pointed. "Let the clay take you."

"I don't think clay works like that," he reacted bluntly, though her touch sent an unfamiliar warmth through him.

By the end of the class, Vivaan's pot looked more like an ill-fitting bowl, but he was smiling for the first time in months.

"See?" Aanya said as she sat down. "You're a natural!"

"It's going to be a natural disaster," he joked, but his smile betrayed his excitement.

One night, a fierce storm swept through the city. Sitting by his window, Vivaan watched the rain lash against the glass. He was startled by a knock at the door.

Aanya stood there, drenched but smiling. "My power's out. Would you mind if I crashed here for a while?"

He hesitated, but something in her expression, a mix of vulnerability and hope softened his resolve. "Come in," he said, stepping aside.

As the storm raged outside, they sat on the couch, wrapped in blankets, and sipping tea. Aanya began sketching on paper, her strokes quick and deliberate.

"What are you drawing?" Vivaan asked, his curiosity piqued.

"Us," she said, holding up the sketch. It was a rough but striking depiction of two figures sitting together, surrounded by swirling winds and rain.

Vivaan stared at the drawing, a lump forming in his throat. For the first time, he felt a connection he couldn't explain, a sense that he wasn't alone.

Over time, Vivaan's life began to change. He started noticing the beauty in everyday moments: the way the sunlight filtered through the trees, the laughter of children playing in the courtyard, and even the simple joy of sharing a meal with a friend.

Aanya's influence was undeniable. She had unlocked something within him, a part of himself he had long buried.

But Aanya, too, found herself transformed. Vivaan's quiet strength and thoughtful nature grounded her, reminding her that it was okay to slow down and savor life's subtleties.

Together, they became each other's anchors, proving that even the most unexpected connections could bring profound healing.

CHAPTER THREE

THREADS OF HEALING

Aanya's apartment was like her personality: colorful, warm, and inviting. Pictures piled up on the walls symbolized vibrant illusions of life and emotion. The fresh coffee brew left a lingering aroma amidst the delicate lavender scent. As Vivaan moved forward, he felt better, although he didn't know why.

"Make yourself at home," Aanya said, waving her hand towards the lumpy couch, casually stacked with mismatched cushions. She vanished into the kitchen and the clinking of cups filled the silence. Vivaan stood there, stiffly gazing around. The building seemed alive with a burst of energy that contrasted sharply with his simple, abstract structured room.

Aanya went back and came with two cups of coffee in them. It was steaming hot. She said, "I hope you don't mind it black, offering him one.

"It's okay," Vivaan said, getting comfortable on the couch. He held the cup very carefully; the warmth penetrated his fingers slowly.

"So, Mr. Enigma," Aanya started, her lips curving into a teasing smile. "What do you do when you're not lost in thought in the elevator?

Vivaan blinked at her softness. "I. work as an engineer," he said, sipping coffee. It was intense, with a hint of cinnamon. He had not expected that.

"Engineer, huh? That explains" Aanya said, nodding toward his usual attire. "But surely there's more to you than numbers and spreadsheets."

Vivaan's lips twitched in what might have been the beginning of a smile. "Not much. Work keeps me busy."

She turned her head to face him. "You know, you're a hard nut to crack, Vivaan. Most people can't stop talking about themselves, but it's like you're hiding something."

Those words cut deep into Vivaan, though: she had not intended to be harsh. He gripped the mug so hard that he did not look at her again. "Some things are better left unsaid," he muttered softly.

Realizing he had made a sensitive point, Aanya decided to steer the conversation to a lighter place.

"Fair enough," she said quietly. "But I'm a good listener if you ever want to talk. And I make decent coffee, too, as you just discovered."

Vivaan looked at her. His face smoothed out a bit. "I'll remember that," he said.

Later that night, while lying in bed, Vivaan couldn't help but think of Aanya. The way she laughed, the way she talked so fast, and the unspoken understanding in her eyes all remained in his mind. She was unlike anyone he had ever met, which fascinated and unsettled him.

Vivaan had a burden he had long buried deep within himself. His life was once full of love and light, but tragedy snuffed out even the brightest flames. He had lost his parents in a car accident years ago. The pain of their absence was unbearable, and after that, he had built walls around his heart, shutting out the world.

A knock such as Aanya's was on those walls. She did not push or pry; however, her warmth went through the cracks, and he wondered whether it was possible to feel alive again.

Aanya, too, found herself thinking about Vivaan more often than she cared to admit. Something about him drew her in—an air of mystery she couldn't resist unraveling. She recognized the signs of a wounded soul; she had seen them in her younger brother, Aarav, when he had spiraled into darkness after their parents' divorce.

Though Vivaan's pain was different, Aanya felt an inexplicable need to help him. She knew better than to think she could do that, not to fix him but to offer a safe space and a moment's respite from whatever weighed on him.

Her art often reflected how she was feeling. During the next several days, Aanya painted a string of abstracts in shades of deep blue and grey, touched with streaks of gold—that reminded her so much of Vivaan: stormy seas and sunshine peeking through the clouds.

Their communication became regular. Aanya would often invite Vivaan for coffee or a walk in a park nearby. To begin with, Vivaan refused but slowly answered "yes" more often. He began spending time with her, and Aanya lightened up about participating.

Walking through the garden one afternoon, Aanya pointed to a wooden bench by the pool. "Let's sit down for a while," she said. Vivaan nodded and sat on the side, watching the sunlight dance in the water. Aanya spoke up after a moment of silence. "Sorry for intruding and getting all private, but is that how you've constantly been quiet? Or is that just reserved for me?"

Vivaan let loose a gentle giggle, which greatly surprised Aanya. "No, it's not simply you," he confessed.

"I have always preferred keeping things to myself rather than talking out," he added.

Aanya faced him and said, "But you see, sometimes conversing does magic. You have a knot, and solving it is the only way out, but you must untie it first, piece by piece."

If the knot is too tangled, Vivaan asked her curiously, "What do you do?"

Aanya firmly stated, "Then you don't do it alone. You allow somebody to aid you."

And as weeks turned into months, their bond grew more assertive. Gradually, Vivaan shared a little about his life with Aanya. He told her about his childhood. Love of classical music and his favorite books. He never talked about his parents death or the pain that fed his loneliness.

Aanya respects his boundaries and doesn't push him away. She realizes that healing takes time and that trust cannot be rushed, so she focuses on being there for him by offering friendship and unwavering support.

One evening, while they were sitting on Aanya's balcony, they watched the city lights twinkle below. Vivaan came up to her. "Thank you," he said in a deep voice.

"For what?" Aanya asked,

"For being you," he said. "For reminding me that there's still kindness in the world."

Aanya smiled, her heart swelling with warmth. "Thank you for letting me in," she said. "It means more than you know."

CHAPTER FOUR

BRIDGES OF THE HEART

One bright autumn evening, Aanya invites Vivaan to her art show. It's a small gathering. The works are deeply personal in a cozy gallery in the city's heart, showcasing her latest collection, Echoes of the Soul, by mixing bright colors with dark undertones.

"I want you to come," Aanya said, her eyes sparkling. "It's nothing fancy. But it has meaning for me."

Vivaan knew he wasn't comfortable with crowds or social gatherings. But he couldn't notice it when he stared into her eyes. "I'll be there," he promised.

When she went on stage, he was amazed by the beauty of Aanya's work. Each painting told a story that combines happiness, sadness, chaos, and calm. One work in particular caught his attention. Blue and grey lines with yellow lines intersect like beams of light.

"Do you like that?" Aanya's voice frightened him. She popped up next to him, her cheeks red with pride and nervousness.

"It's... powerful," Vivaan said openly. "What is this?" he inquired. Aanya says "recovery" is about finding strength in the darkest times.

A few weeks passed by and they became closer collectively.

One night Aanya received a call that her brother Aarav had hospitalized himself after suffering a panic attack. She was restless and wandered around her apartment seeking to figure out what to do.

Vivaan sensed her distress and offered to send her to the hospital. "You don't have to be alone right now," he said firmly as he reached for his car keys.

Along the way, Aanya told him about Aarav's mental health issues. "He's been through a lot," she said, tears streaming down her face. "I just want him to be okay."

At the hospital, Vivaan stayed by her side, offering silent support as she spoke with the doctors and comforted Aarav. His calm presence was a source of strength for Aanya, who realized how much she had come to rely on him.

Once they reached home after a long night, Aanya turned toward Vivaan and said, "Thank you," in a shaky voice. "Without you, I don't know what I would do."

"There is no need to thank me," said Vivaan with a soft tone. "You will do the same for me."

One evening, on their way home from a nearby coffee shop, they suddenly discovered it was raining heavily. They laughed and got soaked. They sought shelter under a small shack. Aanya shook her hair playfully, scattering water droplets into the air.

"You look ridiculous," Vivaan teased with a rare smile.

"Forgive me?" Aanya pretended to feel guilty. "You are a nice person to talk to, Mr. Soakedsuit."

They laughed, mixed with the sound of the rain. But when the smile fades, Aanya notices something different in

Vivaan's expression. That's something weak.

"I haven't laughed like this in years," he admitted in a small voice. "I forgot what it felt like."

Aanya's heart sank when she heard his words. "You deserve to laugh, Vivaan, to be happy."

For a moment, he seemed like he would say more. But he shook his head. "It's not that simple," he muttered.

Aanya placed her hand on his arm. Her touch was gentle but firm. "Maybe not, but you are not alone anymore."

Despite Vivaan's growing feelings for Aanya, he struggled with his past. One sleepless night, he sat in his dark room, looking at an old picture of his parents. The weight of his grief was compressed, constrained, and relentless.

The next day, he appeared at Aanya's doorstep looking disheveled and sad. "I have something to talk about," he said in a serious tone.

Aanya welcomed him in without hesitation, guiding him to the couch. He hesitated for a long moment before finally speaking. "I lost my parents in a car accident. I couldn't help them."

Aanya paid attention quietly, her heart breaking for him. "I'm sorry, Vivaan," she said softly, "and the pain will never go away."

"They are everything to me," Vivaan continued, his voice shaking. "And after they left I don't know how to live. I didn't do that. I just exist."

Aanya had tears in her eyes as she reached out his hand. She said, "You have been holding this alone for a long time. But you don't have to anymore."

At that moment, something changed between them. She understood him and saw who he was.

The more time spent together, the more the bond becomes clearer. Aanya and Vivaan begin to share their hopes, fears, dreams, and regrets. During the conversation, Aanya encourages Vivian to come back to life.

One evening, while watching the sunset from Aanya's balcony, Vivaan said, "You have changed my life."

Aanya said with sparkling eyes, "And you changed mine too."

They slowly leaned in towards each other and kissed gently and willingly for the first time. It's not the beginning of their story. It is a continuation of a new chapter in their journey together.

CHAPTER FIVE

THE JOURNEY WITHIN

Aanya and Vivaan's relationship has blossomed like a spring flower after a long winter. From the moment they met, there was an undeniable spark between them. It was an obsession that could not be ignored. But their relationship wasn't formed in one moment or one big event. The accumulation of numerous small, important interactions brought them closer together.

Their picnics in the park were a particular favorite. Every Saturday, if the weather permitted, they would pack a basket filled with their favorite snacks: sandwiches with fresh, crusty bread, fruits so ripe they dripped with sweetness, and a thermos of Vivaan's expertly brewed coffee. An ancient oak tree's branches sprawling protectively over them would give them a comfortable spot. Aanya loved the way the sunlight filtered through the leaves, casting dappled patterns on Vivaan's face as he leaned back on the checkered blanket, eyes closed in contentment.

Sharing stories, laughing at childhood memories, and dreaming about the future were all part of these afternoons, not just about food and relaxation. Aanya would recount tales of her adventurous younger days, of her solo trips to remote villages where she discovered hidden waterfalls and befriended locals who welcomed her with open arms. Vivaan was willing to share his calmer pursuits, like reading, making handmade furniture, and caring for his garden.

Their quiet dinners at home became another cherished ritual. Aanya, who loved experimenting in the kitchen, would often whip up elaborate meals—spicy curries reminiscent of her grandmother's cooking or creamy pasta dishes inspired by her travels to Italy. Vivaan was determined to be her assistant chef, even though he had no culinary skills. He would chop vegetables, set the table, and occasionally try out the dishes in progress, for which he received playful scoldings from Aanya. "Patience, Vivaan," she'd tease, swatting his hand away with a wooden spoon.

After the meal, they sat around a small wooden table and talked. The flickering light of the lamp added romance to their cozy atmosphere. Their conversation flowed like wine from their eyes. They talked about everything—their hopes, their fears, the books they read, shows they watch—and it was during these times that Vivaan became extremely grateful for Aanya's presence in his life. Her smile, her curiosity, and her constant support reminded him of the happiness he thought he never could experience again.

But it was late-night conversations that sealed their relationship. Weekends saw them returning to the living room after all the dishes had been cleared and the outside world quieted down. Wrapped in soft blankets, with a pot of chamomile tea boiling away on the coffee table, they would still manage to talk deep into the night. Such conversations were raw and unfiltered. They discussed their deepest fears, wildest dreams, and the moments that had shaped who they are. This opened up Aanya's arms before Vivaan; with every single night, Vivaan slowly lowered his defense and found himself telling portions of his soul, which he had concealed for such a long time.

One night, as they sat together on the couch, Vivaan took a deep breath and said, "You make me believe in love again, Aanya." His voice trembled with vulnerability and his eyes searched hers for a reaction. Aanya's heart swelled with emotion. She reached out to touch his cheek, her eyes brimming with unshed tears. "You've always been worthy of love, Vivaan. I'm just glad I get to be the one to show you that."

They slowly leaned in towards each other and kissed gently.

As their relationship deepened, they began to imagine a future together. Vivaan, who had once been too afraid to hope, started to picture a life where Aanya was by his side. He thought about the house they might build together, with a garden filled with her favorite flowers and a workshop where he could create to his heart's content. He envisioned lazy Sunday mornings, traveling to new places hand in hand, and growing old together while still finding new reasons to laugh every day.

For Aanya, the journey was equally transformative. She'd always been fiercely independent, but with Vivaan, she found a partner who respected her individuality while complementing it with his quiet strength. She loved the way he looked at her, as if she were the most extraordinary person in the world. And she cherished the little things he did to make her feel loved—like leaving her favorite chocolates on her desk after a long day or surprising her with handwritten notes tucked into her books.

Their love story was not without its challenges. There were moments of doubt and insecurity, remnants of past wounds that occasionally resurfaced. But they faced these challenges together, with honesty and compassion. They learned to communicate openly, to forgive each other's flaws, and to celebrate their differences. Each hurdle they overcame only made their bond stronger.

In time, Vivaan's pain from the past began to fade, replaced by a profound sense of peace. Aanya's love had not only healed his heart but also inspired him to embrace life's uncertainties with courage and hope. And for Aanya, Vivaan's presence brought stability and warmth she had never known before. Together, they created a life filled with joy, laughter, and love—a life that neither of them could have imagined on their own.

And so, as the days turned into weeks and the weeks into months, Aanya and Vivaan continued to build their love story. Their journey was far from over, but they knew that as long as they had each other, they could face anything that came their way.

Aanya 's love for Vivaan heals a man's heart and can carry him for the rest of his life even though he has uncertainty, courage, and hope. For Aanya, her love is healing the heart of the man she loves. And she could carry him for the rest of his life. Whatever uncertainty, courage, and hope he had.

The seasons changed, marking the passage of time as their relationship grew stronger. They celebrated festivals together, putting together their family traditions into something uniquely theirs.

Holi became a riot of colors and laughter as Vivaan ran around the garden with Aanya, smeared with all colors on their faces. Diwali brought evening diyas to light together in the house, warming it with glow and light. Even simple activities like grocery shopping become little adventures filled with laughter and playful fun.

Aanya encourages Vivaan to follow his desire. And he supported her desires. Vivaan began to work on specific projects, such as a handmade bench for their garden. It is a symbol of their journey. Where they can sit and ponder their dreams together. When he finally gave it to Aanya, she cried. "Perfect," she said, running her fingers over the smooth shaft. "Just like us," Vivaan said, pulling her into a gentle hug.

Together they explored near and far. Every trip is an opportunity to make new memories and discover more about each other. Whether walking the misty mountains or holding hands on a sunny beach, walking through the bustling market is a delight at any time. Some of their favorite trips are spontaneous, where they throw a few essentials in their bags and hit the road with no set plans...

A very low-key journey took them to a beautiful mountain town. In a delightful cottage surrounded by flowers and waving islands. They spent the morning tea on the balcony, the warm mountain air filling their lungs. The afternoon was spent exploring local artisans, tasting traditional food, and walking through the narrow and winding gate. The weather was amazing. The sky was pink and orange as the sun set behind the mountains.

As they lay there under a blanket of stars during the night, Vivaan turned to Aanya and said, "I never thought I would find someone else to make me feel so alive, and thank you, Aanya, for being my light."

He smiled, love shining in his eyes. "And thank you for letting me in, Vivaan. We created something beautiful together."

CHAPTER SIX

Fading Connections

The lab was silent except for the faint hum of the memory eraser as it powered up. A cold, mechanical glow emanated from the device's metal frame, casting long, angular shadows across the dimly lit room. Vivaan stood in front of the machine, his hands trembling slightly as he adjusted the knobs and dials. The wind felt heavier than usual, as if bearing the weight of his decision. This is what it is; tonight, he will release the chains of his past.

Vivaan's gaze drifted toward the small photograph of him and Aanya pinned to the edge of his bench. A day he might never forget. They stood below the shade of cherry blossoms. She leaned on his shoulder and laughed at everything he said. Her eyes were glimmering as if she was the light that could pull him out of the darkest corners of his misery.

He hesitated for a moment. "Will I still feel the same about her?" he whispered to himself, his voice barely audibles in the empty room. The question hung in the air like smoke, curling and twisting in his mind. He knew the answer didn't matter. He had already made up his mind.

The memories of the accident were like a poison that seeped into everything, even his love for Aanya. If he didn't do this, he would never be able to give her the life she deserved.

He reached for the control panel. His finger pointed at the activation button. He was startled by the sudden knock on the lab door. His heart skipped a beat, and he spun around to see Aanya standing in the doorway. She was wearing one of his oversized sweaters. Her hair is pulled back loosely. Her expression was soft but concerned.

"You're still awake," she said, stepping inside. "I thought you were coming to bed."

Vivaan froze, the weight of his secret pressing down on him. "I... I have something to finish," he said, his voice faltering. He moves quickly by blocking the device from her view, but her eyes had already caught the flash coming from the device.

"What's that?" she asked, tilting her head.

"Nothing," he said too quickly. His voice was sharp enough to make her tremble. He immediately regretted, "I mean... It was just a project I was working on. Something that I was testing."

Aanya stepped closer, her brows knitting together. "Vivaan, you've been so distant lately. I understand that you're dealing with a lot right now. You don't have to face it by yourself. Whatever you're going through, I'm here to listen and support you."

Vivaan felt his chest tighten. He wanted to tell her. He wanted to pour out every thought, every fear, and every ounce of guilt that had been eating away at him. But how could he? How could he dare to admit that he was on the brink of erasing the memories that had formed his love for her? She wouldn't understand. She couldn't.

"I can't," he said finally, his voice barely above a whisper.Aanya reached out and touched his arm. Her warmth contrasted sharply with the cold, clinical feel of the lab. "Vivaan," she stated softly, "you don't have to face this yourself. I've always been right here, always here for you when you need me.

For a moment, Vivaan felt himself wavering. Her words were like a lifeline, pulling him back from the edge of the abyss. But then the memories came rushing back—flashes of twisted metal, shattered glass, and the sound of his mother's voice fading into silence. His fingers went to a fist, and his nails penetrated the skin of his palms.

"I can't do this anymore," he said, slowly his voice cracking. "I can't do this anymore. Aanya, these memories, they are killing me. They are killing us."

Her eyes widened. She was quick to realize. "You're attempting to delete them," she whispered, her voice shaking. "That's what this machine is for, isn't it?"

Vivaan looked away, unable to meet her gaze. "I have to," he said. "It's the only way I can move forward. The only way I can be the person you deserve."

Aanya shook her head, tears welling in her eyes. "Vivaan, no. You can't just erase the pain. It's part of who you are. It's a part of what brought us together."

"That's exactly the problem," he said, his voice rising. "I don't want to be defined by my pain anymore. I don't want to carry it around like a weight on my chest. I just want to be free."

"Free?" Aanya's voice broke. "Do you truly believe that this will set you free? What if it removes more than the pain? What if it alters you? What if it alters us?"

Vivaan turned back to the machine, determination in his voice. "I've already made up my mind," he said firmly. "I can't keep living like this."

Aanya moved in closer, taking hold of his arm. "Please, Vivaan," she begged, "don't do this. We will get through this together. I love you, and I don't care how heartbroken you think you are, you are enough for me."

Her words pierced through him like knives. But it wasn't enough to stop him. He gently pulled her hand away. Then he repented. "I'm sorry," he said, his voice barely above a whisper. "But I have to do this."

Aanya froze, tears streaming down her face. As Vivaan walked back to the machine and sat down on the chair. The electrodes were tied to the side of the head. The cold metal was pressed against his skin. It caused a shiver to run down his spine. He took a deep breath and swiped the activation button.

The machine whirred to life, a low hum building into a high-pitched whine. Vivaan felt an unusual warmth spread across his skull. Followed by a sharp electric current, images began flashing before his eyes—memories of the accident, his parents' laughter, and the time he was in the hospital. He clenched his teeth, preparing himself as the machine started working to separate and nullify the impact.

But then something went wrong. The hum of the machine grew louder, almost deafening. Sparks flew from the control panel, and the light flickered wildly. Vivaan's eyes snapped open, but his vision was blurred, the world spinning around him. He tried to move, to reach for the emergency shut-off, but his limbs felt heavy, as though they were weighed down by lead.

"Vivaan!" she said, Aanya's voice cutting through the chaos. She was beside him, shaking him, with a terror on her face. "What happened? Vivaan, talk to me!"

He opened his mouth to speak. But no words came out. Those images flashed before his eyes began to change. He saw Aanya—her smile, her laughter, the way she looked at him when she thought he wasn't paying attention. And then, one by one, those memories began to fade.

"No," he tried to say, his voice barely a whisper. "Not her, not Aanya."

But it was too late. The malfunction of the machine had taken away not only the pain but also the memories of the one who helped him heal. His vision went black, and the last thing he heard was Aanya's voice calling his name.

When Vivaan woke up, the lab was quiet again. The machine was dark, its lights extinguished, and the faint smell of burnt circuitry lingered in the air. In pain, he forced himself upright, his head throbbing, as well as his thoughts. Near him knelt Aanya. His head was throbbing, and his mind was filled with fog; tears streamed down her startled face.

"Vivaan," she began in an unsteady voice. "Are you fine?"

Looking very confused at the question, he stared at Aanya

He met her gaze, his brow furrowing. "I... I'm fine," he said, his voice unsure. "But... Who are you?"

Aanya's face folded as she swallowed her choked-up sob. "No," she whispered. "No, no, no."

Vivaan turned around and looked around the room and his confusion grew stronger. He felt himself missing something; a piece of him seemed to have been carved away. But he couldn't wrap his head around what it was, no matter how hard he tried.

"I'm sorry," he said finally, his tone apologetic but distant. "Do I... know you?"

Aanya didn't answer. She couldn't. All she could do was watch as the man she loved looked at her with the eyes of a stranger.

CHAPTER SEVEN

PIECES OF YESTERDAY

The scent of vanilla filled the kitchen as Aanya tried to flip stubborn pancakes. Standing next to her, Vivaan practices faking his voice, full of exaggerated power.

"You see, the whole trick is in the wrist," he announced as he took her palette knife.

"Oh, really?" she playfully asked, wrapping her arms around him. "Because the last time, your pancakes ended up on the floor."

"That was a well-planned sacrifice," he remarked playfully, allowing her to have laughed uncontrollably. Her laugh was resonating in the ears in their small apartment. They are surprised by the method of changing Saturday morning as usual into a precious memory.

This had always been their style. The small instances, the day-to-day experiences, seemed enormous because they experienced them together. Their love thrived, nourished by the laughter and peaceful moments they created. Aanya never questioned how strong it was.

But now that sureness was falling apart. It began in small ways. Vivaan's laugh seemed more polite than real when she joked about their "pancake mess-ups." He ignored it at first, but other things followed—he forgot a restaurant they often went to; he paused when she mentioned their favorite song. Each slip felt like a small stone dropped into her heart, making waves of worry.

The time her doubts turned into fear happened one night at the dinner table. "Do you remember when you burned the pancakes, so the fire alarm went off?" She asked, trying to sound casual but hopeful.

Vivaan looked confused. "Did I? That doesn't sound like me."

Her fork stopped moving halfway to her mouth. "You can't recall?"

"No," he replied, shrugging with a bashful grin. "Perhaps it's one of those things that's grown bigger in your mind over time."

Her spirits fell. The joy that had filled their house was now just a faint memory. She looked into his face, but the warmth she knew so well was obscured by something new. Vivaan wasn't withdrawing emotionally. He was forgetting.

Aanya sat cross-legged on the floor, where there was a tide of photo albums and trinkets surrounding her. She ran her finger over the frame of a picture of their initial Goa trip. Vivaan had his arm wrapped around her shoulders as they grinned at the camera, with the sea glistening behind them.

"Do you recall this day?" she asked, handing him the photo. Her voice shook with hope.

He looked at the picture. "That's me," he spoke slowly. "And you. But." He shook his head, returning it to her. "I have no idea where this was."

Aanya's heart broke a little more. She forced a smile. "It's all right," she whispered, though the weight in her chest made it hard to breathe. "It'll come back to you."

She immersed herself in the role of a caregiver, trying to bridge the widening gap between them. She played his favorite songs, took him to their favorite café, and even recreated their first date—an impromptu picnic at the park. But nothing seemed to jog his memory.

One evening, she brought him to the hill where he'd proposed under a sky ablaze with stars. She had worn a red dress that night, and he had kneeled on one knee, his voice trembling as he asked her to be his forever.

Now, standing at the same spot, Aanya's heart ached with longing. "Do you remember this place?" she asked, her voice trembling.

Vivaan looked around, his expression thoughtful. "It's beautiful," he said.

She waited, praying for recognition to dawn in his eyes, but it never came.

The stars seemed dimmer that night.

Vivaan woke in the middle of the night with a dull ache in his chest. He couldn't explain it, but he felt as though something important was slipping through his fingers. Aanya's face flashed in his mind—her laugh, her tears, the way she looked at him with so much love it made him feel invincible. Yet it was as if the well of memories they had made together had a curtain cast over it.

He found himself rummaging through the closet, driven by an inexplicable urge. Hidden at the back was a wooden box he didn't recognize. Inside were objects that felt significant: a dried rose petal, movie tickets, a pressed flower, and a silver bracelet engraved with the word "Always."

He turned the bracelet over in his hands, the word pulling at a part of him he couldn't reach. Always. The weight of it pressed against his heart, heavy with meaning.

As time passes Vivaan's liking for Aanya also increases. Every conversation with her felt both familiar and foreign. He noticed the way her eyes lit up when she talked about books or mumbled under her breath when she thought no one was listening. It felt right to be near her. Even though he doesn't quite understand.

But the frustration of not remembering eroded him. He wanted to give her the reassurance she deserved, to tell her that their love was still there, buried beneath the haze. Instead, he maintained silence, afraid of breaking her heart further.

"Do you even care that I'm here?" Aanya's voice trembled as she paced the living room. Her eyes, usually so soft, were stormy with anger and pain. "Do you know how hard it is to keep showing up, hoping for something—anything—to remind me of the man I fell in love with?"

Vivaan stood frozen, guilt pooling in his stomach. "Aanya..." he began, but she cut him off.

"Do you know what it feels like to watch you look at me like I'm a stranger?" Her voice broke, and tears spilled down her cheeks. "I'm trying so hard, Vivaan, but I don't know how much longer I can do this."

He took a step toward her, his chest tightening. "You think I don't feel it too?" he asked, his voice low but intense. "This...void? Every time I look at you, it's like I'm chasing something I can't catch. But I don't want to lose you, Aanya. I can't."

Her anger faltered, replaced by exhaustion. She sank onto the couch, burying her face in her hands. "Then maybe you should stop chasing," she whispered.

Silence hung heavy in the room. Then, quietly, Vivaan said, "Aanya, that bracelet in the box—it's yours, isn't it? The one that says, 'Always.'"

Her head snapped up, her tear-streaked face filled with surprise. "You found it?"

He nodded; his voice unsteady. "I don't remember everything, but... I know it matters. You matter."

CHAPTER EIGHT

THE VOID BETWEEN

Aanya held onto the hope that her presence and comfort could add some relief to Vivaan's life by reducing the heavy burden of his sorrow. Still, days went by, and his behaviour didn't change—a strange, almost indifferent man towards her as if she were a stranger whom he had somehow forgotten. Each such instance of his cold detachment was piercing Aanya, and it became unbearable for her to deal with his indifference. She had almost lost hope that she could help Vivaan heal. She felt detached, not knowing how to reach out to him, how to bring him out of his pain, or even if he wanted to be saved.

The calm in the apartment lay heavy, thick as the dust particles swirling in the single beam of sunlight splitting the unclean window. Aanya rested on the edge of the shabby velvet chaise lounge; its bright crimson edge stood out against the weak coating of her calm manner. Vivaan, the man she'd thrown her heart to, the man who'd steered her days with laughter, who'd whiled away her nights and whispered sweet jokes into her ear as they lay under a star-spread sky—gone. Not that they are dead, of course. He sat in the next room, asleep or maybe just numb, a shadow of the man she once knew. The Vivaan she loved, the Vivaan who'd held her hand, kissed her forehead, and painted flaming sunsets with words, was gone.

Empty eyes that were once filled with thrilling intensity. Now it seems that the distant galaxy is retreating into darkness. All the warmth and comfort were stolen. Leaving only a cold hole reflected in the unspoken words. Aanya examined the edge of the broken teacup. The floral pattern is a reminder of shared breakfast and the closeness weaving through the world. Even ordinary people now feel alienated. In a place he doesn't know

He'd been different after the surge. The humming of his machine, once a background melody to their shared life, had morphed into something contrary, a stranger. He'd been different after the surge. The humming of his machine, once a background melody to their shared life, had morphed into something contrary, a stranger. He withdrew himself, creating a barrier of silence and staring blankly. As their happy exchange of moments unfolded, they left behind a cold, monotonous sound that chilled her to the core. It seemed like he didn't know her anymore.

She remembered the day they met, the way the sunlight had caught the gold in his hair, and how his eyes, initially guarded, had softened at her laughter. Now, in such fragrant solitude, the scent recalled in all its strong detail was his—A scent of rain-soaked earth and a touch of ozone now lingered, ghostly and ethereal, clinging to her like a shadowy memory. Those memories were like leaves swirling in the winter wind, sharp and precious yet so fragilely threatened to be blown away by forgetfulness.

Then there was the light that struck him like a blow from his body; he would never remember any of it. All their histories together, all those stolen kisses under the stars, all the dreams of the future—these were gone. It wasn't just a matter of forgetting; it was as if nothing had ever transpired between them. The thought of all his memories being erased was unbearable, as if someone from the past had come along and scrubbed them away, reducing significant moments to nothing more than data.

One tear rolled down, as if it were the only river navigating this devastated landscape of grief. His indifference weighed heavily on her, as if it were squeezing the air out of her. She was not mourning just lost love; she was mourning the destruction of a life they had built together, a past they had shared, and a future that would never be.Now, it stood as a touching reminder of their lost love, a delicate light against the growing shadows.

Choosing to leave is inevitable—a silent surrender to the harsh reality of their situation. The rest could only vent their feelings of unease. As she watched Vivaan's confusion, he became confused and disconnected day after day. A determined effort to free her from the void in the tomb that threatens to consume her. She carefully packed a small suitcase, selecting only the essentials: a few changes of clothes, a worn sketchbook, and a handful of photographs captured in time.

Every photo was a wound, reminding her of the past shared between them that had just dissipated into thin air, much like morning mist. And it was with those memories that she clung to the Vivaan she loved, refusing to let go of the Vivaan she knew.

Before departing, she put the red flower in a small, dark red glass vase, leaving him without fear of the monochrome landscape of her suffering. It is a quiet witness for their love story. The signal of hope reminds us what it is. A testament to the power of love in that moment, no amount of distance or even twisted machinery can truly erase it.

The apartment felt strangely empty despite the lingering scent of him, a haunting reminder of a love that vanished too soon. As she stepped out into the cool night air, the city lights blurring into a distant hum, a sense of intent settled over her. There was an undeniable ache in her heart, a hollow void that mirrored the emptiness she'd seen in his eyes. But down in that darkest recess of her spirit was a persistent ember of hope, fostered by the intense memory of his smile and the enduring fragrance.

The streets seemed to stretch out before her, endless and unknown. But she walked forward, each step a testament to her resolve and her resilience. She carried her memories like precious jewels, shielding them from the harsh realities of their lost connection. She would find her way, find her path, but the red poppy, a powerful symbol of their lost love, would remain forever etched in her heart, a silent witness to a love story that defied the very fabric of time and technology.

Days turned into weeks, weeks into months. Aanya immersed herself in her art, using her brushes and paints to translate the turbulence of her emotions onto canvas. The red poppy became a recurring motif, its vibrant crimson petals a metaphor for the enduring power of love, and its delicate fragility a reflection of its vulnerability. Each painting was a testament to her grief, a cathartic release of her sorrow, a journey of self-discovery.

She travelled, seeking solace in the changing landscapes, the unfamiliar faces, and the ever-evolving horizons. But the shadow of Vivaan, the echo of their shared laughter, remained a constant companion, a bittersweet melody that played on the strings of her heart. She found comfort in the rhythm of her work, in the act of creation, in the act of bringing beauty to the world. But the absence of him, the void left behind, was a constant ache, a reminder of their story's abrupt ending.

She received no word from him—not a single call, not a single message. The silence, as unforgiving as the void that had replaced their shared existence, enveloped her. Yet she held onto the memory of his touch, the feel of his hands in hers, the warmth of his embrace. It was a lifeline, a connection to a past that science had tried to erase but love had stubbornly preserved.

The red poppy, not only a symbol of their lost love, turned out to be a symbol of her resilience, of her strength. It represented the unwavering power of the human heart, the ability to love deeply, to grieve deeply, and to resist any adversity with hope. She grieved the loss, but she did not give up hope. Part of her had thought that one day their paths would cross again, and their story might find its way to a different conclusion. At the heart of the storm was a whisper, a hope that wavered slightly against the darkness of the meeting. The poppy was a silent promise, a symbol of a love that technology had tried to destroy but could never fully erase, a beacon in the dark, waiting for its moment to shine. It was a love story that was not yet finished; it was merely paused, suspended in time, awaiting its next chapter.

The Color of Nothing

The years stretched out endlessly before Vivaan as some gray terrain. The colours of life with Aanya had faded. He was alive, technically, but the essence of living had vanished with his memories. The machine that had been used as a way to find solace had taken much more from him than the grief of losing his parents. It took away from him a vibrant piece that would echo laughter, whisper secrets at the quiet of dusk, and the casual perfume of Aanya on his clothes.

His days were now a ritualized repetition of actions performed without feeling. He got out of bed, ate flavorless meals, worked in his laboratory—a space that had once been alive with creativity, now a sterile symbol of his defeat—and slept, only to wake up to the same sense of emptiness. The lab reflected his mental state: dusty tools lay scattered among incomplete projects, a physical representation of his disarray.The soft hum of his machine echoed his ambitions and the painful results they had produced.

He attempted to focus on his work, which had previously given him joy and intellectual stimulation. However, the equations now seemed like mere symbols, lacking the thought that had once fuelled his passion. He continued making social appearances. He went back to attending various reunions hosted by former coworkers. Again, it was meaningless conversation, laboured smiles on laboured faces with hollow words repeating into the gigantic hole of what was lost by keeping his memories of that time shut off. He was a ghost in his own life, a spectator who could only watch a world he could no longer understand.

His apartment transformed from a warm shelter to a shut-off and cold unfamiliar space. The photos that once captured moments of joy are lifeless and devoid of color. Now they are mute, and a constant reminder of the past he doesn't have access to. He also got rid of all his old clothes that bore her scent and replaced them with neutral-color attire that blended into the grey landscape of emotions. Each garment became a sensory trigger too painful to bear. He couldn't even play his favourite albums that marked significant moments with her. He couldn't bring himself to hear them now. Every note reminds him of the moment that is now boycotted.

All he was offered in place of reality was a new one, where the fragments of faces and emotions brought him a step closer to the life he desperately wished to live. Yet, so far away. These dream fragments were elusive, dissolving like smoke as soon as he attempted to grasp them, leaving him feeling even more hollow upon waking. The world around him continued its remorseless rotation, but he moved through it as if submerged in a thick fog, his senses dulled, his emotions muted. He still existed, physically. But his soul existed somewhere far off. There, slowly drifting away. Silently. Loosely.

He reasoned his actions away, carefully monitoring how his thoughts chose thier paths to avoid psychological torture. Yet a flash would still surface, filled with unnamed, painful desires. Perhaps it was a faint echo of a life once known—a life so full of love, laughter, and diverse connection that it could only be fondly described as 'a pulse'. Occasionally that soul would ripple, and the closest feeling to describe it was life itself.

Such moments may come when he found himself blankly staring at red objects that still caught his attention. A fire truck? Or poppy flowers? Indeed, some sharp sting of pain would satisfy him, piercing through with an irredeemable ache he was forced to endure.

These fleeting sensations, though elusive, served as a harsh reminder of what he'd lost and of the profound emptiness that still resided within him. His work habits, once detailed and specific, became unsteady; his attention often went aimless. He found it hard to focus, his thoughts wandering to vague sensations—the feel of Aanya's hand in his, a soft laugh, a shared gaze. These fleeting images only strengthened his sense of loss. He started to avoid places he and Aanya had frequented—the quiet park where they picnicked, the bookstore where they had browsed for hours together. He didn't go near the cafe where they had their first date. Instead, he confined himself to the familiar, predictable routine that had come to be in the absence of anything else.

The absence of emotion wasn't merely a lack of joy; it was a chilling absence of anything at all. Anger, frustration, even sadness—all were absent, replaced by a flatness so profound that it felt like a vacuum where his feelings once resided. He was a shell, walking through the motions of life, devoid of genuine passion or purpose. The world, once filled with color and vibrancy, now appeared monochrome. The sounds of the city, once a chaotic yet pleasing symphony of life, had become jarring and excessive—a symphony of reminders of the silence in his soul. The once comforting rhythm of his life was shattered; now he stumbled from one day to the next, caught in an excessive, lifeless present that offered no hope of the future.

He attempted to analyze his emotional state, employing the same scientific hardship that had guided his work on the memory erasing machine. He kept meticulous notes, documenting his moods, his physical responses, and his increasingly unsteady thought patterns. He hoped to find a logical explanation, a scientific solution to his problem, as if he could cure the void using the same techniques that had created it. But his efforts were fruitless. The problem was not a mechanical one, something to be calibrated or repaired with scientific precision. It was a human problem, one that defied his attempts at objective analysis.

Even the simple act of eating became a chore. The flavors of the food were dulled, the textures unfelt. Each bite was taken not out of hunger or pleasure but simply because Vivaan's body required fuel to maintain its skeletal structure. There was no joy, no anticipation, no satisfaction. His life had become a series of devoid activities that he performed out of duty rather than genuine desire. It was a life lived half asleep, existing in a state of perpetual numbness. Even his dreams, which once carried pieces of his relationship with Aanya, now become barren, devoid of color and substance. The dreams are not dreams anymore; they are merely black-and-white snapshots of empty spaces.

He wondered whether he was truly alive. Was this what existence felt like without love, without memory, without the vibrant hanging of human connection? The question hung in the air, unanswered, a constant reminder of the profound void that had come to define his life. He was a monument to his failure, a ghost haunted by the absence of a past he couldn't recall, a present he couldn't feel, and a future that seemed hopelessly out of reach. The red poppy, a silent testament to a lost love, became an imagined vision—an illusion image he often tried to recollect. The image never came back to him in its entirety. Only a trace of red was left against an endless, gray sky. That is what his existence was like. It was a tiny speck of a color against the infinite, colorless expanse of nothing.

CHAPTER TEN

BETWEEN MEMORY AND HOPE

Aanya's studio was filled with the comforting scents of flaxseed oil and paint thinner. Sunlight streamed through the high, arched windows, illuminating the dust particles floating in the golden beams. Years had passed since the disastrous power surge, since the cold void had settled over Vivaan, leaving her heart burdened with a grief so intense it seemed ready to engulf her. The red poppy, a fragile symbol of love violently torn away, remained a persistent motif in her work, a silent testament to a loss that ran deeper than words could express.

Her early paintings after Vivaan's disappearance were a swirl of chaotic strokes, a tempest of color reflecting the storm within. Deep crimson, like poppies, merged into purples and blacks. These colors were visceral and raw, vividly portraying the anguish of a love twisted by fate, a love eternally plundered by a machine meant to heal. Critics deeply engaged with the pieces called it a powerful shift into profound expressionism and raw emotion. The initial confusion of being taken aback by the sudden style changes did not go unnoticed.

However, Aanya was blinded by the cracks in her own heart. Each brushstroke suspended the tears unshed, and every canvas was a mute scream. Each canvas slowly began to reveal the agony that was buried within. The poppy they once saw was buried in the posted stamp of her memories. With every stroke, echoing sobs became less acute. The stern boundaries began to soften, and the colors started to melt together, filling her with the deep sense of tranquillity. Strands of crimson began to blend with new shades—twilight lavender, calming blue, and the soft golden glow of the fading sun.

Now their meanings have moved beyond loss. The poppies, still elegant, had transformed into a symbol of quiet contradiction. The art drifted away from the raw agony in real-time and instead remained on distant echoes, faded memories whose whispers stay between colors.

She started to add other images portraying the inner battle for stability. Poppies and landscapes started to shift into geometric shapes—straight lines and sharp corners. These elements signified her attempts at external control over internal chaos—attempts at building a new structure on the ruins of her past.

The landscapes shifted from being dry and barren to being filled with life, beginning with the surrealistic mountains set against deep and vibrant skies. These were not fantasies but subtle traces of hope coupled with a gentle weave of strength and courage.

Her work now became a sort of visual diary, tracing the reflux and flow of her grief and her slow, painful journey toward acceptance. One of the pieces titled "Transient

Blossom" was a poppy, all red against deep midnight blue. The poppy had been drawn very sensitively: its petals, seemingly fragile, contrasted with color that seemed to shout vibrancy and life against all the darkness. The colors are contrasting, she thought, for her feelings. The deep blue reflected the vacuum of Vivaan's absence, always reminding her of what she had lost, while the bright red was her fighting spirit to hold on to her memories, her love.

The second artwork, "Broken Reflections," made use of cracked mirrors to convey fragmented memories. Among the shattered pieces, there were glimpses of light and hints of the poppy. The disjointed images mirrored the scattered state of her recollections with Vivaan, representing the doubts that clouded her future. The poppies, however, remained constant, suggesting that even the deepest wounds can reveal beauty when given the time to heal. These weren't merely paintings; they were fragments of a soul attempting to rebuild itself. They were whispers of her journey—a journey of healing and acceptance, a transformation both beautiful and heartbreaking.

Aanya's artistic journey was a testament to the power of art to transcend pain. It was an intimate exploration of loss, resilience, and the enduring strength of the human spirit. Each brushstroke was a step forward, each canvas a milestone in her healing process. She kept Vivaan in her heart; she didn't try to erase him from her mind. Instead, she turned her suffering into artwork, weaving it into a colorful mix of memories, sorrow, and careful steps toward a future she was building bit by bit. Her work attracted attention not only for its aesthetic beauty but for its profound emotional resonance.

Art critics lauded her ability to capture the rawness of emotion and her honesty in confronting difficult times.

She received numerous awards and accolades; her work has been exhibited in prestigious galleries around the world. But these successes were a step to the actual development of her inner self. It was not about seeking glory or even approval; it served a purpose—to heal, to find serenity in the mess, to turn pain into something beautiful. The red poppy, once a sign of ultimate loss, grew to become that symbol of persistent strength, a constant reminder that even in the darkest days of life, art finds a way to flourish. The achievements didn't bring comfort or satisfaction, though.

She found no comfort, no satisfaction in her success. The clapping, the awards, and the good reviews all felt hollow, like a pointless melody in a world where the brightest sound was gone. Vivaan's absence resonated in every gallery, in every soft murmur of admiration. She felt oddly isolated among the throngs, surrounded by fans, yet deeply alone. Her art, so celebrated by others, was a personal act of grief, a tribute to a love that felt irretrievably lost.

The colors used to show her inner confusion, but now they seem more like a self-made pretty trap. One night, after a great tiresome gallery show, Aanya found herself solo in her art space. The usual comforting smells of turpentine and flaxseed oil just made her feel alone. Her hands, with paint all over them, reached for a new canvas. The blank canvas mocked her and reminded her of the hollow inside. She stared at it and thought about what to paint next. What new things could she express? How could she get her art to speak when her own insides were so silent? The red poppies that used to stand for hope are now in pain. They had a ton of weight on them, a heaviness even their bright color couldn't fix.

She dipped her brush into a palette already saturated with the reds, blues, and purples of countless other paintings, shades mirroring her own emotionally complex journey. Moving without thought, she laid down a daring swipe of crimson, followed it with more, and soon a bunch of poppies came to life on the canvas. But this time, they were different. There was a hesitancy in her brushwork, a subtle uncertainty in the lines.

She didn't paint the poppies like the bold, bright ones she used to. This time, they looked softer, not as loud in color—kinda gentle, you could say. And then something unexpected happened. In with the flowers, she starts sneaking in thin silver streaks, like a glinting net thrown over them. Those silver lines twisted through the petals, tying all the poppies into this big web. She got it then; those lines were like the bond she's got with Vivaan. These invisible ties hung on spanning years without a word closing the gap they had.

Her memories bloomed like poppies, with the silver strands representing a connection that not even time's flow or tech disruptions could break. Instead of grieving through her artwork, she was confirming her belief in ongoing affection and recognizing a tie that no gadget could wipe out. This new painting showed that there had to be some change for her. It was not just a reflection of her sad story but rather presented hope in this endless love.

It was a painting about memory and about the constant strength of the human heart to heal, to forgive, and to believe in the possibility of a future that had seemed impossible. The red poppies still held their vibrant color. Still, now, they were interlaced with threads of silver, representing the enduring connection that defied the limitations of time and technology, a silent acknowledgment that even in silence, love persists. Her artistic journey had reached a new stage, a stage marked by not just grief but by hope, a stage where she painted not just her pain but also her faith in the future. A future where she could still see the flicker of a red poppy—a memory of a love that neither time nor technology could ever erase.

CHAPTER ELEVEN

ECHOES OF SILENCE

The Grand Gallery was filled with a low, expectant buzz. Crystal chandeliers flickered, scattering light across polished marble floors, and the silent, expecting faces of the art world were assembled. The air vibrated with the gravity of anticipation, the fervent odor of costly perfume mixing with the highest sense of antique paintings.

Aanya flickered the top of her profession with a retrospective that encapsulated a decade of inventive progress, a journey she fashioned through heartfelt sorrow and the slow emergence of desire. The exhibition, titled "Echoes of Silence," became a formidable announcement, a proof to her toughness and her ability to transform pain into something beautiful, something enduring.

Vivaan stood near the long wall, almost hidden among the crowd of elegantly dressed buyers. He came almost by mistake, drawn by a unique strength—a whispering behind the brain, a half-memory that pulled him like a lost thread. He was not an art specialist. His world was one of balancing with cold precision in engineering. Still, he found himself fascinated by brilliant energy radiating from the canvases, each stroke speaking volumes, whispering stories that he could not understand.

The crowd participated in a moment, revealing a painting that stopped him in his tracks. It was not a grand, broad landscape or a dramatic picture. It was still a life, simple yet developed deeply.

A single, vibrant red poppy canvas, its petals in an ideal bloom against the background of muted grays and blues. Yet, poppy seeds had no representation of a flower. It pulsed with an inner light, a quiet intensity that resonated with a deep emotion within Vivaan's being. He recognized it instantly, not as a conscious memory but as a feeling, a visceral reaction that bypassed his intellect and spoke directly to his soul. It was the poppy Aanya had left behind years ago; a soft goodbye engraved in his ruined memories.

He felt a tremor pass through him—a small shift in the scene of his lost past. A dam inside him seemed to start breaking, a surge of buried feelings ready to spill over. He moved closer, looking at the soft brush marks, how the light danced on the fine texture of the petals, and how the painter had caught the true nature of the flower, making it more than just a basic plant.

These weren't full scenes or clear memories, but more like feelings, reflections from a past life that had been wiped away but not gone. They were the fragments of a love that had burned so terribly it left a mark on his soul, a mark that even the technological void of memory erasure couldn't entirely wipe away.

He felt a sudden tightness in his chest—a combination of pain and hope. The void that had tortured him for ages started to break, unveiling a slight hint of familiarity, a soft echo of memory. This gradual, painful resurgence was both agonizing and emotional, as he emerged from a quiet, barren place into a world where emotions, even if broken, still existed.

For him, the gallery became submerged in the depths of his imagination. In its place, the relentless pulse of his emotions took over. The atmosphere in the room changed, coming to a pause. A calmness settled over the gallery. His imagination, boundaries of the painting; all of its emotions raised. All the lost memories that were like fragments of a mirror were slowly coming back together, helping him to put the pieces back together.

A soft and hesitant voice broke through his dream. "You... you seem drawn to that one."

He turned, his heart leaping into his throat. Aanya stood in front of him, looking even prettier than he recalled, her eyes showing the same kindness and smarts that had drawn him in years before. Her hair was arranged in a fall of curls, framed by a face engraved with both intense sadness and tentative hope.

Her eyes, which used to shine with excitement, now convey a depth of experience. She gained her knowledge through many years filled with silence and loss. Nevertheless, the spark persisted—a flicker of recognition that confirms a bond has endured the challenges posed by time and technology.

He opened his mouth to say something, but words wouldn't come. He was trying to piece together all the disconnected memories that had been overflowing into his mind and settle them with the reality of Aanya being there. The years of silence felt like an eternity, a vast gap that seemed impossible to overcome.

However, when he thought back to that moment, he recognized that the difference wasn't as significant as he had believed. The red poppy on the canvas, now a mute observer of their love, became a link between them. He came to understand that his spirit was remembered in ways that science could never truly capture.

"I... I don't know what to say," Vivaan finally managed, his voice with a rough whisper.

Aanya smiled with a bittersweet expression that said a lot. "I think we both have much to discuss and many memories to cherish." She paused, her gaze fixed on the painting, on the red poppy that appeared to vibrate with a hidden past.

"This poppy," she said softly, her voice holding slightly. "It's... it's a little bit about you, Vivaan."

He stretched out, and his hand trembled as it reached out to hers. This touch was like a slash of lightning through his body, an honest manifestation of powerful bonding, which he shared with him—the bond that survived years of silence, loss, and intervention from technology.

The machine had failed to erase their love. Their souls still held onto it. In the stillness of the Grand Gallery, surrounded by the echoes of a life only partially remembered, their story began once more, a will to the lasting strength of the human spirit, the resilience of love, and the inability of technology to erase something as deeply human as memory and connection.

He saw the painting that brought him together and felt that his story was just the beginning. This was a difficult break in the years of isolation, but even red poppies, once a symbol of their loss, now stood for their love. It is shown that their relationship cannot be broken, not even by time or technology.

The gallery buzzed with activity, unaware of the important reunion happening right there. But Aanya felt like a weight had been lifted from her shoulders. She and

Vivaan shared this moment, rekindling their love and hoping for a future where broken things could be fixed.

The painting "Echoes of Silence" was not just a work of art; it was the proof of a love story as enduring, the type that could withstand the wounds that were scientifically impossible to heal. But even the red poppy could spark their love.

The show, "Echoes of Silence," took visitors on a trip through. Aanya's creative journey, showing how her feelings looked on canvas. Every piece of art told a part of her tale, moving from deep sadness to a small spark of hope in her heart. Her early works had dark, gloomy colors, showing her raw pain and how much Vivaan's sudden distance hurt her. These pieces were marked by sharp lines, a sense of fragmentation that mirrored the fractured state of her memories, and the unsettling feeling of a world turned upside down.

The timeline of the exhibition demonstrated a change in colors, getting warmer and livelier as the exhibition progressed. The sharp lines that once made up the image gave way to smoother brush strokes hinting at a slow healing and a careful return from dark times. Landscapes made an appearance and pointed to a comeback to life, the outside world, and simple pleasures once out of reach.

The final section of the exhibition displayed pieces created in recent years. These were different; they were infused with a newfound sense of peace, of acceptance. The colors were deeper and brighter, but not flashy or celebratory. They showed quiet self-assurance, recognizing the hardships faced while also seeing the good in even the toughest situations. Throughout the exhibition, like a persistent theme, the red poppy appeared, evolving in its symbolism, mirroring Aanya's transformation.

The poppy represents a sign that the love that they had gone through has passed the time constraints and technology restraints, creating a connection over time and innovation. Its bright color and its fragile beauty stood out against the soft shades of her past works, reminding people how the human spirit can find hope even when facing deep loss. The poppy served as a silent observer in their love story, linking the past to the present. It intertwined the heartache of being apart with the joy of coming together, demonstrating that love can thrive even in moments of silence.

The final artwork, a large canvas painted with red poppies and streaks of silver, summarized the exhibition. It was a bold declaration, a striking reminder that love, like a resilient flower, can thrive despite life's obstacles, with its roots deeply anchored in our core, unwavering and strong. The silver lines weaving through the vibrant red acted as a touching representation of the enduring power of the human spirit, the strength of love, and the truth that love persists even without words.

UNVEILING THE PAST

The paintings hung at the back of the gallery, crammed together in a dim corner near the rear, almost hidden among those more abstract ones. It didn't matter so much about size; most of Aanya's other works had been larger statements. It hadn't been anything to do with technique, but the brush strokes were undoubtedly hers—an almost intensive energy captured in the way the paint was applied. No, it was the subject matter; something very evidently moved him, which pulled at a deep ache in his being, a lost chord resonating in the stillness of his soul.

A field of red poppies, bathed in the soft shine of the sun. The poppies themselves were presented with an energy that was almost lukewarm with life, their crimson petals glittering with an almost spiritual glow.

Aanya had captured the subtle variations in color and the delicate textures of the petals with a precision that was breathtaking. But it was more than just technical skill that fascinated Vivaan. It was the emotion, raw and unfiltered, that throbbing out of the canvas. The feeling of longing, loss, violent and delicate love filled the place around the painting and stuck it as a phantom coupling.

He stood ahead, fascinated; his breath was sticking to his neck. A strange energy caught him—a close urge to feel the texture of the paint under the fingers. The memories that have been idle for years stirred within him as if the spark suddenly ignited the flame. Flickers of life he once experienced passed by in his brain: the scent of rain soaked on the sidewalks, the taste of cheap wine drunk on benches under a parky night, or sound of distant laughter echoing throughout the summer night. These fragments were brief, confusing, and yet undeniably familiar, each fragment carrying the unsteady but clear essence of Aanya.

The red poppy. Aanya held a single, bright red poppy in her hand as she turned away, and the memory came back to him. It was a shattered memory, yet it felt so real. He could see her tears, hear her quiet words, and feel the crushing weight of his forgotten love. He remembered the deep sense of loss, a breach revealed in the landscape of his memory. The painting wasn't just a depiction of poppies; it was a mirror reflecting a forgotten reality, a visual echo of a love lost and then, miraculously, found again.

The vibrant crimson stood out sharply against the grey emptiness that had haunted him for years, a hollow created by his own invention, one he had foolishly thought he could fill with ignorance. The painting stood as a testament to the enduring power of love, a strong reminder of a connection that had transcended the boundaries of time and technology. Even though his machine had erased his memories, it could not erase the intense mark Aanya had left on his mind.

He leaned in to study the details of the painting. There was a fine detail in the lower left-hand corner—a small silver locket hidden amongst the poppies. One he hadn't noticed earlier. It was almost identical to the one Aanya used to wear—a tiny silver circle that contained a faded photograph of his parents.

A photograph, strangely enough, that seemed amazingly alive in the reconstructed memory within his mind. The locket, a symbolic thread between his past and his present, was a tangible connection to the love he had lost and the memories slowly, painfully coming back.

A wave of discomfort washed over him. He felt the familiar drag of emotion—a raw, powerful blend of joy and pain, of relief and fear. The long years of silence and the deep pain that had surrounded him do not hurt him anymore. The heaviness of his loss, once unbearable, was light enough to carry on his own shoulders. The feeling of hope, almost delicate but undoubtedly, began to bloom in him.

He pulled out his phone, his hands shivering slightly. He needed to find her. He had to. He felt a belief that would shake off logic—that he had to find Aanya. His memories were returning, slowly, timidly—but they were returning. And with them came the desire to reconnect with the woman who had at one point filled his life with color and light and who had haunted the edges of his consciousness for years.

He found her name, Aanya, listed in the exhibition catalog. It was a small detail, yet it was enough. He had a starting point. He had a thread to follow. He had a reason to hope. He scrolled through the digital gallery catalog and found a contact email address linked to a website promoting her upcoming exhibits.

He looked at the email address, his heart throbbing out an anxious movement against his ribs. This was it. This was his chance. He had to be careful in approaching her gently and respectfully, remembering that he had lost years of their shared history. How would he explain his sudden reappearance? How would he explain the blank space in his memory? How would he explain the unexplained revival of his love for her? He knew that his return would come as a shock, a seismic shift in her life, as it was to his. He had to think about the conversation in his mind before speaking with her.

He headed for the exit of the gallery, yet in his mind, the image and emotions of the painting stayed. The fiery red poppies, representing a love that he nearly lost to time, now stood there as a sign into a future he couldn't even imagine yet. A future there, despite the fear of time and their technology—functional errors—their love power remained unchanged. His love was not a program that could easily be removed. There was a complex algorithm in the heart, which was a biological miracle beyond the understanding of any machine.

He inhaled deeply. The atmosphere in the gallery brightened as the burden of his grief began to fade. He found a fresh wave of energy, purpose, and hope that had prevented him for so long. This was not just about bringing back memories; it was about taking back his life, his love, and his future.

The red poppy, painted in bright colors against the gray of a stormy day, throbbed in his imagination. It was not just a flower; it was a key, released to unlock secret chambers of the mind closed long ago. The first shock had come immediately, like a stinging prick that took away his breath. Now, a rising flow of memory crawled up, tugging him deeper, carrying with it bits of a life long forgotten.

He remembered flashes: the laughter that echoed in a sun-kissed café, the touch of Aanya's hand in his, the scent of her perfume—a combination of jasmine and vanilla that now stays in his senses—a whisper of a feeling he couldn't quite hold on to.

He thought of her eyes, of how they creased at the corners when she smiled, of that smile once that had once been the light in his dark world. These weren't fully formed memories; these were echoes, bits of melody played on a broken instrument, disjointed notes hinting at a beautiful lost song.

The next few days were a confusion of intensive burden. The painting became a passion; Vivaan found himself back to the gallery repeatedly, standing before hours, lost in the spinning loops of re-emergence. With each visit came more pieces: the taste of her favorite chocolate cake, the sound of her voice, soft and melodic, reading poetry aloud in their shared apartment—an apartment he couldn't quite picture but whose existence he now felt with absolute certainty.

Memories didn't come in order; they arrived in random, disordered, and incomplete bursts. A flash of laughter shared on a rainy day, the warmth of her hand in his while they crossed a busy street, a stolen kiss under a sky full of stars. Each memory experienced a deep desire—a powerful sense of loss linked with pure joy, the bittersweet sensation of something almost retrieved.

Sleep became a confusing area of fragmented dreams, reality and fantasy entangled, where the boundary between past and present blurred into a single, indistinguishable fog. He had a dream of Aanya's face, vivid, while at others a ghostly phantom was seen just beyond the edge of consciousness. He woke with a gasp, his heart pounding; even though the feeling was gone, there were still the ghostly fingers of her touch on his skin. What once was his companion in silence was now filled with sound echoes of a life he could not remember perfectly but desperately wanted to know.

The red poppy, the recurring theme in Aanya's painting, became the anchor in this violent sea of rediscovery. He began to notice red poppies everywhere: in the photographs pasted on magazine covers, in flower arrangements at the cafes he dropped into, even in the designs of fabric prints people wore. There were hints and whispers scattered down the path, drawing him nearer and nearer to the memory he longed for.

He found Aanya's email address and carefully crafted a message. It was short and to the point, avoiding any grand pronouncements or explanations. He stated his name and mentioned the art exhibit. He said he had been inexplicably drawn to her painting of the red poppies and was eager to meet with her to discuss her art. It was a carefully constructed message, avoiding any mention of their shared past or the machine.

He sent it, then just sat there holding his breath with a tense hold in his manners. He waited as he stared blankly at the screen, the expectation and unease circling together in his mind.

What was she going to say? Remember him? Write back?

The questions hung in the air, unanswered, heavy with the weight of unspoken emotions, a proof to the vulnerability of reconnecting after years of painful silence.

He waited, feeling the silence stretch on, each second feeling like an eternity. His phone buzzed finally, breaking the nervous tension. He knew instantly, before even opening the message, that this was Aanya's reply. His heart pounded in his chest, a drumbeat of anticipation accompanying his rapid pulse. His hands trembled as he opened the message. He read and re-read it, each word setting off a storm of emotions. He smiled slightly, a slow, tentative smile that expanded until it lit up his face. Aanya had responded.

CHAPTER THIRTEEN

A LOVE REBORN

The gallery was almost empty, the silence only interrupted by the rhythmic ticking of a clock in the distance. Vivaan found himself in front of Aanya's latest work, a vast landscape featuring a striking red poppy at its centre. The memory came rushing back, vivid and intense: Aanya, laughing with a single red poppy placed behind her ear. A shiver went through his body, reminding him of the time he'd lost and the emptiness in his life he still needed to fill. The painting wasn't just a flower picture—it showed their story together, honouring a love that survived its flawed beginnings.

He spotted her address in the gallery's guest book, written by hand next to a typed name. The address took him to a small, plain cottage on the edge of town. The place seemed alive with quiet energy, showing the creativity and warmth of the woman, he knew—or rather, the woman he was starting to remember. He walked up, his heart beating fast against his chest. He felt excited and nervous at the same time, making his throat feel tight.

He paused, his hand close to the old wooden door. Time had left marks on his face, but his eyes looked brighter now. His love for Aanya had come back to life, putting a new spark in them. He knocked, the sound echoing in the stillness of the evening. He listened, holding his breath, praying that the years hadn't changed her too much and that the woman who stood beyond this door was still the woman who had stolen his heart, a woman whose laughter had once filled his life with a joy he had almost forgotten.

The door squeaked as it opened, and Aanya appeared. Time hadn't been kind to her; the passing years had left their mark, carving lines of grief near her eyes and giving her posture a tired look. Still, the vibrant glow in her look, the same appealing energy that had first attracted him, stayed bright. It seemed as if time had frozen, keeping intact the core of the woman he cherished. The red poppy, an ongoing symbol of their shared history, showed up again in her artwork, her daily life, and the soft curve of her grin.

"Vivaan?" she whispered, her voice just above a breath, a mix of doubt and hope. The name, unused for years, felt strange yet familiar, echoing in the depths of his heart that had just woken up. Her eyes, big and inquisitive, looked over his face, trying to find answers to the questions that they both now dared to ask.

He nodded as feelings washed over him. The word seemed too small—a weak attempt to close the gap of time they'd lost. He wanted to say so much, to explain everything, to apologize for the pain he had inflicted, but the words seemed to catch in his throat, choked by the huge flow of his revived feelings.

He drew closer, the faint but clear smell of sandalwood infusing the air between them. It was a scent he would have thought they had left behind, one that kept holding to the sounds of their laughter, their sneaky kissing, and the promises they never made. It hinted at a love that had survived the effects of time and the flaws of machines. He reached out to her, his hand shaking a little as he gently touched her cheek, his fingers tracing the soft lines around her eyes—a silent reminder of the years that had gone by and the journey they both had experienced.

"I... I remember," Vivaan tried finding the right words to speak. "I remember it all."

Aanya had to pause to collect her breath. Although tears fell from her face, reflecting the warm light of the candle, it was those tears that were relief and joy. They showed the huge impact of a much-awaited reunion and a hoped-for acceptance. She moved closer to his touch. Her body shook a bit, showing years of unspoken yearning and the delicate hope that had at last turned into reality

That silence was indeed full. Filled with unaccounted words that were absent for far too long. It was a true testament to their shared stories. That had bound them together and became unexpressed feelings. He pulled her in close, and the warmth of her body poured over him. That love was genuine. And that love had indeed overcome the storm.

They spoke for hours, their voices barely above a whisper as they pieced together the fragmented memories, the lost years, and the silent pain that had separated them. Vivaan admitted his regret, his guilt over creating the machine, and the sadness that had driven him to erase the pain of loss, only to lose the love that had been his relief. Aanya spoke of her heartbreak, of her confusion, and the quiet sorrow that had threatened to consume her in the wake of his sudden change.

She recounted the days after the incident, the distressing confusion as she attempted to navigate a reality removed from his presence, the red poppy, a silent tribute to their lost connection. Her voice was filled with a mixture of sadness and forgiveness, a witness to the depth of her love, a love that refused to be erased by technology or time.

Vivaan listened closely, absorbing every word, every insight of emotion, his heart sore with a heavy sense of regret yet filled with the growing hope of a future where he could make things right, where he could rebuild their lives together. He learned about her struggles, her artistic growth, and her resilience amidst the devastation of their lost connection.

They spoke of the painting, the red poppy, as an emotional symbol of their enduring love, a testament to the strength of the human spirit, and a stubborn refusal to surrender to the harsh realities of loss and heartbreak. They spoke of the years apart, the silent longing that had fueled their journeys, the unwavering hope that had kept their love alive in the depths of their hearts.

As dawn approached, painting the sky in shades of soft pinks and oranges, they sat together, hand in hand, their shared silence more expressive than any words could ever be. The scent of sandalwood, a constant reminder of their past, filled the air, an actual link between the past, the present, and the future they were now building. The red poppy, a symbol of strength and enduring love, blossomed in their hearts, a testament to love that had survived the test of time, the flaws of human nature, and the limitations of technology.

The reunion was not a simple act of remembrance; it was a process of healing, of forgiveness, and of rediscovering the depth of their connection. It was a testament to the enduring power of the human spirit, a strength that transcended the boundaries of time and space. This love challenged the strategies of technology, a love that only now was being truly understood, appreciated, and celebrated.

Their journey had been long, difficult, and filled with pain. But in the caring welcome of the rising sun, a new chapter began—a future painted with the vibrant shade of love, a future where their hearts were whole again. They had lost years, but they had found each other again, and that, they knew, was more than enough to begin. The red poppy, a symbol of their enduring love, served as a sign of hope, guiding them towards a future filled with love, forgiveness, and the unbreakable bond that technology could never erase.

CHAPTER FOURTEEN

THE LOVE THAT STAYS

The atmosphere between them was electric, not in the usual sense, but with a delicate, uncertain energy. Years had passed, creating a gap formed by Vivaan's self-induced forgetfulness. The reunion, though filled with joy, had also revealed a terrain of emotional debris. The vibrant, free-spirited Aanya that he recalled was a woman who had watched all his memories fade.

She gently placed the teacup back on the saucer. The quiet sound mirrored the storm of emotions rising within her. The Aanya who was able to loosen gleeful joy from her eyes now emerged as a figure of stability and quiet rage. Even though the silence was not awkward, there was a shared understanding that they were trying to walk the tight rope that reconstructed the fragments of their interlaced lives, all shattered by a faulty machine at the end.

"It's. different," said Vivaan, shaking his voice and unsure of himself. He felt like what he was saying wasn't good enough, as if he was trying to connect the dots between who he was at that point versus who he is now. He remembered the bright spark of their first meeting—the way they fit so easily into each other's arms.

As she slowly nodded her head, Aanya's look remained fixed on the steam rising from her cup. "Different," she said as if it were heavy. "But... not bad. Not entirely bad."

He recalled, feeling a flicker of the brightness, he remembered in her, how a smile played on her lips. Those following weeks became a painful process of rediscovery. As they spoke endlessly, he learned everything about her hurtful struggles. He pieced together the suffering that ended from his unreasonable withdrawal, along with the sadness that was hidden to drown her as he drifted further away. He listened and allowed his mind to be filled with the memories that had haunted him for an eternity.

Every shared memory felt like a precious gem pulled from the ruins of his forgotten past. He noticed their shared joy reflected in her look and could hear traces of her voice on his own. The red poppy, a constant reminder of their broken bond, turned into a real connection between their different paths. This red poppy is what he could see in the patterns of her last paintings, which were expressions of her feelings and mental state.

The conversations weren't always easy. The silence, the unspoken questions, the lingering pain of what was lost—these hurdles demanded patience, understanding, and a willingness to confront the ghosts of their past. Vivaan's activity sometimes caused deep frustration, threatening to break their fragile connection. Still, Aanya's quiet resolve served as a solid foundation during tough times.

He learned to understand her complex emotions and how she was able to forgive. It was not just about letting go; it was more about the strong bond between them and their mutual commitment to building a future together. He was aware that his sudden departure had caused pain on her, but he had also begun to praise her actual strength that enabled her to navigate through those difficult times.

Meanwhile, the machine sat in his lab silent, a cold monument to his vanity. He examined its construction to look for fault rather than necessarily to fix it. As he explored the power surge, he found out there wasn't an electrical mistake at all. But it revealed that there was a basic flaw in the machine's design—it showed how impossible it is to eliminate emotion fully with technology. The machine could erase memories, but it could not erase the love that remains in the soul.

Though the sorrow had been taken away, something from him and from Aanya remained. A small essence of that love, which acted as the base, had survived the modesty of the machine. It reflected on a much deeper and more basic level, a core of his identity. His subconscious was holding onto it more fiercely than he was aware, a connection the machine could not recognize.

His investigation also led him to a deeper understanding of the human brain, the resilience of memory, and the complex dance between experience, emotion, and the very essence of self. The machine had only scratched the surface, dealing in raw data and digital code. It couldn't account for the intangible, the deeply personal, or the fleeting nature of love that transcended the physical and digital realms.

It took him on a journey to understand himself—a deep self-analysis of the profound strength of human relationships. This showed the limits of scientific knowledge and celebrated the unbeatable human spirit. He wanted to wipe out sorrow, but this process instead brought him face-to-face with what love means—a deep insight that went against his first plan, showing the core of what makes us human.

His work with the machine wasn't just about exploring science; it dealt with how such technology affects our feelings. The emotional void he felt served as a strong caution, showing the moral issues that come with messing with the human mind.

He now understood the complications of human memory—its resilience, its ability to heal, and its relationship with trauma. He discovered that memories are not just data points in the brain; they are complex, emotional narratives that shape who we are and influence our choices. The machine, in its simplistic manner, had failed to recognize this deep truth.

He published an article on the limitations of his machine, which included warning the public of the ethical implications of memory alteration. He was lauded for his honesty in admitting the unintended consequences of his invention. His forthrightness stunned the scientific world and is the turning point of the ethical debate regarding memory modification technology.

In the evenings, as the city lights glittered below their apartment window, Vivaan and Aanya would sit together, their fingers interlaced, sharing not just memories but dreams. Now, the future looked brighter with their love as a shield against their past grievances.

A future filled with renewed hope, their resilient love never transformed or deepened into something more intense, unlike the rest of the world. Their love was more than technology; it was intelligence and emotion combined along with passion. Their love challenged and destroyed all boundaries. A love that once set the world in a frenzy of hatred was now rekindled and set anew like a phoenix emerging from the ashes. Rebirth and existing without boundaries set by the world—that was the power of their love.

The red poppy that symbolized the loss now signifies their love, which stands the test of time, indicating the passage through which they have crossed. It celebrates the love that has been strong enough to withstand the huge impact of the digital age. It remained a symbol of hope and strength and a witness to the power of love, one that could never fade no matter how smart science would get.

The scars did remain, but they were deeply connected with the beautiful threads of their reignited love, blending out their future, moment by moment. The failure was of the machine, not the love, and in that victory parallel with the love came the future.

CHAPTER FIFTEEN

CHOOSING US

Aanya inhaled deeply, her fingers gently brushing against the edge of Vivaan's hand while she looked out at the horizon. The sky was a stunning blend of twilight colors, with dark purples fading into warm orange streaks, as if the universe itself had taken a moment to witness this scene.

"I never thought we would reach this far," Aanya said softly, with a wide smile. "There were times when I really felt like the universe was trying to keep us apart." Vivaan just looked at her, his eyes full of depth and emotion that couldn't be expressed in words. He held her hand tightly, grounding them both, as if to assure her that this was all real.

"I know," he admitted. "There were days when I questioned if we were strong enough and if I was strong enough. Every time I thought about giving up, I realized—I couldn't imagine my life without you. Despite how challenging it felt, I knew I had to keep fighting for us.

Aanya met his eyes, searching for the rest of their past challenges. She had witnessed numerous sleepless nights, misunderstandings, and pain. But above all, she had seen the love that never failed as everything around them tried to collapse.

"We've fought so much," she said quietly. "Against expectations, against misunderstanding, against our fears. Vivaan smiled softly, shaking his head. "And yet we have." His stare crossed the distance between them with a hint of a grin. "Here. Still ourselves."

A soft laugh escaped Aanya's mouth; the sound carried a relief and a touch of disbelief. "You make it sound so simple."

He smiled, brushing a loose strand of hair from her face. Perhaps love was never about winning or losing or proving anything to anyone. Maybe it has always been about you and me choosing each other over and over.

The tears in her eyes were not of sadness; they were of deep gratitude to have made it through. She had long feared love would not be enough. However, standing beside Vivaan made her feel like love was the only thing moving them forward.

"Today, and every day after that, I choose you," she said with a confident warmth in her voice.

Everything else disappeared from the mind at that moment. The moment brought them pure joy because no worries or difficulties from their past pursued them. Every heartbeat within them pumped with the promise of affection, which extended into eternity.

Aanya let herself lean back while bursting into laughter by shedding tears from her eyes. There were moments when you considered the differences between us might be too big to keep our relationship going.

Vivaan smirked. "Oh, we are different. That's undeniable. When it comes to planning details, you take control, while I choose to keep things spontaneous. You enjoy peaceful evenings with a book, while I crave the excitement of being outdoors. Still, we somehow found a way to fit together."

She nodded, wiping at her eyes. "Somehow, we do."

"Because love isn't about being the same," he added thoughtfully. "It's about wanting to understand each other, even when we don't. It's about finding harmony in the chaos. And honestly?" He grinned. "I wouldn't change a thing about us."

Aanya tilted her head. "Not even the fights?" she teased.

He chuckled. "Okay, maybe I'd change a few of those. But only if it meant we still ended up here, together."

She smiled, leaning into him. "I like the sound of that."

The night deepened around them, but for the first time in a long time, there was no rush to move forward, no need to fix anything. They had already won the most significant battle, choosing each other despite everything.

Vivaan exhaled, his arms tightening around her. "So, what now?" he asked playfully. Aanya looked up at him, her eyes twinkling with the same hope she had carried all along, even when she hadn't realized it. "Now? Now, we begin again. Not as two people fighting to stay together, but as two people who finally know that nothing can break us."

He nodded, a slow, satisfied smile spread across his lips. "Together."

She squeezed his hand, stepping closer. "Together."

As the wind whispered around them, carrying away the reminders of their past struggles, they stood in perfect harmony, knowing that whatever the future held, they would face it side by side. Because love, in its purest form, had always been enough.